Caterpillar Dreams

Written and illustrated by
Clive McFarland

HARPER
An Imprint of HarperCollinsPublishers

Library of Congress Control Number: 2015958390
ISBN 978-0-06-238636-6

The artist used Caran d'Ache Neocolor II and Winsor & Newton watercolors
on 98 lb Canson Mi-teintes paper and merged them in Photoshop
to create the digital illustrations for this book.
Typography by Rachel Zegar
16 17 18 19 20 SCP 10 9 8 7 6 5 4 3 2 1
❖
First Edition

With special thanks to Rachel Zegar,
who designed this book

Henri has a dream.
He wants to fly.

His whole life, he's wanted to see the world
outside his garden.

Night and day, Henri dreams of going on amazing, incredible, impossible-seeming adventures.

But Henri is just a little caterpillar.

And how is a little caterpillar ever going
to see all that the world has to offer?

His friends don't want Henri to leave the garden.

"It's safe here," says Snail.

"It's where your friends are," Worm tells him.

"Seriously, Henri, an adventure? Sounds exhausting," Slug says with a sigh.

Only Toad understands. "Here's the thing with dreams, Henri. If you don't chase them, they always get away."

Henri is determined not to let his dreams get away.

"Hi, Bird. I want to go on an amazing, incredible, impossible-seeming adventure. Will you take me?"

"I'm waiting for my eggs to hatch, but I can help you get over the wall," sings Bird.

"Perfect," says Henri.

But on the other side of the wall is a busy road.

"Hi, Mole. I'm going on an amazing, incredible, impossible-seeming adventure. Can you help me?" asks Henri.

"I can't go on an adventure today. I need to finish my tunnel under the road," Mole mumbles.

"That's okay. I'll help," says Henri.

But on the other side of the road is a big, big lake. "Hello, Fish. I'm going on an amazing, incredible, impossible-seeming adventure. Want to come along?"

"Oh, I could never leave my lake, but I'm happy to help you across."

"Awesome," says Henri.

Henri flew over a wall, burrowed under a road, and crossed a lake—but still, his adventure had barely even begun.

Then, far ahead, Henri sees something he's
never seen before—a giant balloon.

"THIS is where my amazing,
incredible, impossible-seeming
adventure will begin."
Henri just knows it.

If he can get to the top of the balloon, Henri will be able to see the whole wide world!

But before Henri reaches the top, something
happens to him. A cocoon starts to form around
him. He tries to wiggle and squiggle his way free,
but he can't move.

Henri is stuck. His dream is going to get away.

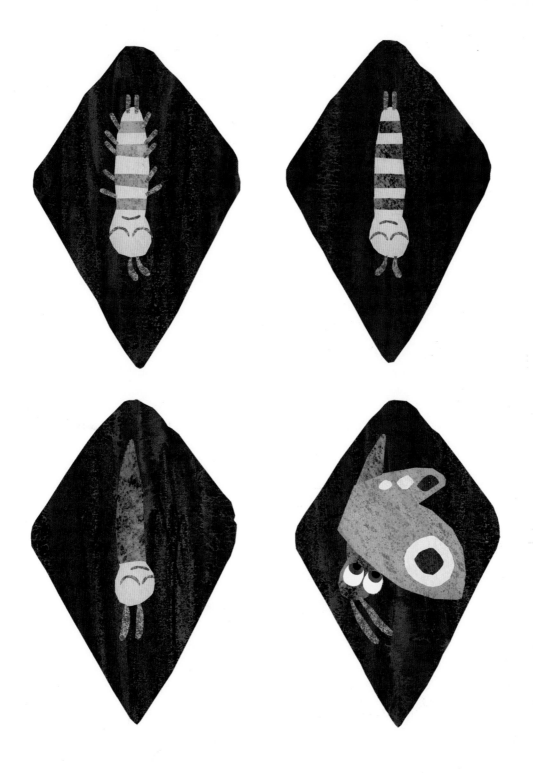

It is dark in his cocoon, and warm. Henri can't
help but fall asleep. But while he sleeps, something
happens that is more amazing than any dream.

Henri wakes and pokes his head out of the
cocoon. He is riding the balloon, high in the sky.
Henri knows he should be scared, but he isn't.

Henri has become a butterfly.
He has wings.
He can fly.
He can go anywhere. . . .

So where does Henri go?

Home.

The most amazing, incredible, impossibly possible place of all.

Never stop chasing your dreams.